Co

Ly ... Brown

For Jennifer, although she may never read this.

Preface

Cream and Blue,

I remember you.

Cream and Blue,

Much too coo.

Cream and Blue,

What are you gonna do?

When the dogs begin to howl.

Cream and Blue,

I got a tattoo.

Cream and Blue,

I got it for you.

Cream and Blue,

What am I gonna do?

When the dogs begin to growl.

Cream and Blue,

I remember you.

Cream and Blue,

We loved you too.

Cream and Blue,

What are you gonna do?

You're a Phantom on the prowl!

I'm a gorgeous cat named Blue.

People always tell me, especially my caretakers. I refer to them as white-skinned monkeys. They're big and slow, and cradle me and ask in a voice reserved for babies:

-*Who's* so gorgeous? *Who's* so gorgeous?

Who's the gorgeous kitten?

You are. *Yes, you* are!

Yes, you are!

They always want to know what I'm doing, especially the taller, rougher monkey, named Sid. He comes home from work and takes off his clothes down to his underwear. Then lies down next to me on the bed, where I enjoy the last of the afternoon sun. He looks lovingly in my face and asks in a soft voice:

-*What* are you doin'? *What* are you doin'? *What* are you doin'?

This continues for the next five minutes.

He also tries petting me, but he's clumsy.

His breath's sour. He needs a shower.

I nibble at his finger as a warning, but he never takes heed. I swat a few times without nails and then gently rake his arm.

Anymore petting and I strike with claws.

I give him a lingering death stare and relinquish the bed.

It was heaven in the sunshine until he arrived.

They gush all over me; I'm spoiled.

I live in a big, old house that the monkeys keep clean.

The gentle one's the first thing I really remember.

Her name is Victoria- not Vicky, not Vick, certainly not Tori or any other variation or nickname.

She wrapped me in her old black and white T-shirt and I fell asleep in her arms.

I could tell by the worn cotton and smell, that this was an old, comfortable, favorite and now it's mine.

When we reached the house, Buddy awakened me.

He's the fourth member of our family, a pug.

The monkeys have a thing about flat-faced animals because I too have a flat face and large eyes. I look like a Persian, but I don't have that obnoxious long hair.

My hair's short and sleek. I'm gray, but the cream accents blend giving me a light blue hue.

Sometimes the monkeys say I look like a ghost glowing in the dying light of a winter's day. They fancy themselves poets.

They named me Blue.

Buddy's blonde, has a black mask, and curly tail. He's sweet but dumb and difficult to tolerate at times.

I remember his bulging eyes peering at me as Victoria lowered me close to his flat face. He panted. His tongue hung loose from his dopey smile. He was so excited; his tail whirled like a propeller and he danced in place. He moved in to have a sniff.

I was a 6-month-old kitten, but I let him know he was rude.

-Holy shit, she's fast!

Said Sid as he pulled Buddy away just before I took out his eye with a violent spit of the claw.

-She's scared.

Victoria whispered in a knowing way lightly pushing the boys aside.

Her long, dark hair smelt nice. Her warm breath cooed me to sleep.

I still curl up on that black and white T-shirt.

I always curl up with Victoria.

After a week of hiding under the monkeys' bed, I felt comfortable.

2

I'm nocturnal.

I'm the best hunter in the world.

If I were larger, I'd eat Sid, Buddy, and even Victoria, but I'm only eight pounds.

I settle for swatting them, attacking their feet, and sometimes rubbing up against them when they least expect it.

Sometimes I stare at them when they're sleeping.

I imagine tearing out their throats.

Don't blame me. If you have a cat, it thinks the same way; it's our nature.

But, we must concede to the dominance of our caretakers, even if they're bumbling monkeys. Besides, I have plenty of living creatures in the big, old house to keep me amused.

I like to explore the dark sections of the basement and attic. I'm at home in the dark.

The attic's fun because of the spiders and open space. Sometimes I launch swatting at the fat buzzing bluebottles in the summer.

But it gets too hot. It's my #3 favorite hunting ground.

The basement's made of fieldstone. The foundation's over a hundred years old and hasn't budged in all that time.

I feel alive when I ascend the shabbily carpeted steps. The damp smell's full of a whole new world compared to the rest of the house. My senses are full bore by the time I silently pad across the concrete floor.

Everything becomes clear, slows down, opens up.

I sense the entire room:

a dripping water pipe, slight smell of mold, concrete pebbles in my paws, living creatures beginning to breathe again after falling deathly silent.

I'm a goddess.

I usually hop up the oil tank and make my way to the makeshift wooden rafters.

I'm most comfortable peering down.

I settle silently and wait.

I'm a stone. I'm precision.

I'm taking in the entire hunting ground, my #2 favorite.

I can see a few small insects milling about in the corner. I hear a fat June bug buzzing but it's outside. I examine the dog food stored underneath the stairs. Occasionally pests sniff nervously observing the impossibility of opening the large bag. Tonight it's silent.

Most of the giant stone structure's quiet. The pipes and electrical wires run along the raw wood ceiling and rafters. They emit a slight hum.

The large room's used for laundry and storage. There's also an area with tools, workbench, and table.

I make my way to the boiler pipes and slowly shimmy along the length of the basement ceiling.

As I approach the end, I hop up onto the conjoining stonewall of the next room.

It's long and narrow and much darker than the larger room. It has only one small window that opens to the driveway.

I wait.

Hunting is patience.

Buddy and the monkeys don't know patience.

Buddy sleeps, sniffs for the smallest morsel of food, and constantly demands attention.

Sid and Victoria don't even kill the spiders they find in the house. Usually Sid coaxes the arachnid onto a paper towel.

Then as if he's carrying a stick of lighted dynamite, tiptoes to the backdoor and throws it into the night. I follow and sometimes try to sneak outside, but they always keep a sharp watch on me.

I'm a prisoner in this old house. I'm an indoor cat; Victoria reminds me. I sulk resting my head on the shelf of one of the dining room windows.

It's beautiful.

It's a dream.

It's my #1 hunting ground and I have never been on it.

I study the colors and life that appear before my eyes. I try to push my way through, but the thin glass prevents my outdoor hunting campaign.

So I sit and wait. Patience. I know patience.

I sit on the wall for a few hours in the quiet. I can't help glancing out the small window. It's bolted shut, but the shadows blowing in the breeze and the constant summer insect sounds hypnotize me. I blink my eyes and turn away only to find myself drawn back to the outside.

My ears twitch. I hear a spider- two spiders, the Daddy-long-leg variety.

I'd like to hold out for a better trophy, but the sun's approaching. Once the sun's up, I fall into a deep sleep for hours. I prefer sleeping on the living room couch instead of the damp basement.

I take action.

I pounce and the force throws them; I'm too rough. Most of their legs are broken and twitching, twitching, twitching. I'm hypnotized.

I pull the closer one apart and spit out the acrid remains. I prefer tastier game, but once the kill-switch is thrown, I can't stop.

The second spider puts up no fight. I amuse myself jabbing at the death throes of each long leg.

I head back to the main floor to clean.

No trophies, the prey wasn't worth it.

I leave two houseflies at the far end of the antique dining room table that I nabbed prior to venturing downstairs. I eat at the other end.

I feast on "crunchies" out of an ergonomically correct ceramic bowl. The table is well used, but the black walnut top gets polished daily.

When Sid notices my trophies, he'll reward me with a small piece of bacon. It's the best thing I've ever tasted every time I taste it. I'll scarf it down and begin to growl anticipating Buddy's frantic charge for the precious treat. I really can't blame him; the smell makes us shiver.

I enjoy sleeping. It takes control and pulls me under. I dream of vast green grass. I lie in the shade. I soak up the warm glow around me.

My belly's full and I've no fear.

I've an urge to purr- softly. I purr deeper splitting the vibrations into multiple sounds. It pulls me under further. The sleep wraps my lungs while the thousand purrs in my skull and frame soothe bones and cartilage.

Sometimes I feel like I can control my dream. I can get up at any moment and do something. My head twitches and I spread my toes. My slender body goes rigid. It's a crossroad, but I always choose slumber, and I really don't mind at all. My body goes limp and I plunge into the sweetest oblivion.

3

I smell coffee. I hear running water. The closet doors open and close. I smell shampoo, soap, shaving cream, perfume. It's the daily morning assault on the senses. As they rise, I sleep.

Now I'm victim to the morning news on the television- It's so dramatic and strange.

Yawns. Sneezes. *Bless yous*.

I endure the morning rush to bask in the serenity of the afternoon.

Sid misses my daily offering of kills. That's okay, I'm exhausted and don't feel like dealing with Buddy. He's asleep on his back in the middle of the living room under the large whirling ceiling fan. His pink and brown belly bulges between his four blond legs pointing half-crooked to the ceiling. Any decent hunter knows never to leave the soft vulnerable belly exposed. I debate whether to pounce and teach him a lesson or allow the comical nap to continue. His tail wags. I leave him to his dreams of eating garbage and sniffing butts.

I can't help but listen. My ears are always open.

I can't help but watch. I'm always alert.

I can't help but smell, extract information. Sometimes I regret this gift, especially when Buddy's sensitive skin gets itchy. Then he smells like a cheese.

I can't help but touch. My whiskers sense the slightest vibration. The sensitive hairs guide my periphery.

I can't meow. I don't know why. Maybe I have nothing to say, but it helps me skulk. The best I can do is a deep purr and a spit or hiss when I'm rankled.

I saunter upstairs to wake Victoria.

I gently hop up the low platform bed. The mattress is that space-age foam. The texture always catches me and I have to give it a sniff and gently prod before padding onto Victoria's chest.

I rise and lower to the rhythm of her breathing. I rest my head on my front paws and purr. She opens her eyes.

-Hey.

She rubs the back of my ears and under my chin. My body goes limp and the purring doubles. I relax and peer at Victoria through slit eyes. I love this. The scratches and pets send ripples through my body.

She begins to rise and it's all over too soon.

She heads for the bathroom; I collapse on the space-age foam in the sun.

Sleep.

4

I'm awake. I stretch. Sid's engine turned the corner.

He kills the motor, slams the door, and walks gravel footsteps. The driveway is crushed cinder and the sound makes me long for a good kneading with my paws.

I shake and head down to say hello.

I bop downstairs and see him bending over Buddy waking him up.

-Yep. Always the best guard dog. Thanks Buddy.

Sid says sarcastically to Buddy's tired sad eyes that suddenly shine because the monkey's home.

-Hey Blue. Now you *are* a good guard kitten.

He says extending his pinky squatting down to say hello.

I sniff the finger. Then I drive my face into it. The pinky slides between my eyes just above my nose up to the first knuckle. It gently wiggles as I push and pull. It feels amazing.

When the pinky is removed, it has some black gunk on it.

I sniff and lick.

Sid wipes the remains on his wrinkled chinos, rises, gets Buddy's leash, and they are off for the afternoon jaunt. The uncivilized beast doesn't have the stuff to even begin to master the toilet.

I walk to the box on the back porch and have a piss. The door slams and they are gone.

Sleep.

Its late afternoon and the shadows are getting long. I eat more "crunchies", lick and clean.

I hear Buddy scratching at the door. He beats Sid to the backyard once his leash is released. He can't wait for his reward.

I wait on the cool kitchen counter.

Sid rewards Buddy with a treat, throwing one my way as well. I struggle to pick up the morsel due to my flat, near convex, face and fat cheeks. I finally scoop the snack into my mouth and prance off triumphantly with my thick tale in the air.

I sit in the kitchen window and watch Sid.

He turns on the ceiling fan and opens the crank window, so I can get a sniff of fresh air. The first inhalation, I'm filled with light, sounds, colors, smells. I reestablish my spot and stare at the outside world.

After an hour, Victoria comes home. I meet her at the door.

-Ah, the queen is home, hey kitten?

Sid says when he sees me trot to the door.

I sit. She scoops me up and carries me upstairs telling me about her day.

-Kitten. You won't believe the idiots I work with…

She stops to kiss Sid two or three times. They always kiss hello and goodbye.

She continues a rundown of her day. I hang on every word.

Victoria's voice is naturally low and soothing. Its music- the cadence, annunciation, change in pitch. It's amazing.

I watch her change. She talks all the while. Her movement captures me.

Suddenly I'm running down stairs. I slide on the smooth wooden floor to see chicken. Ground chicken! My head bobs in excitement. Sid is making chicken tacos!

Buddy charges around the corner after I receive a nickel-sized piece of raw chicken.

Poor Buddy, he's always a step behind. He has to wait while Sid stirs the pan and moves to the cutting board. He eventually gets a half-cooked piece, Ha! The raw is so much better.

The heady smell of Mexican food fills the kitchen and makes its way to the dining room. I'm on the table devouring another piece of chicken.

Victoria and Sid talk and cook.

Buddy grovels.

I take a drink and head for the litter box.

Clean.

Victoria and Sid eat at the dining room table. They enjoy their food and I like that.

Buddy walks from one side of the table to the other hoping for something- mainly food, but any kind of attention is appreciated. He wines softly.

He's pitiful, but it works. Sid feeds Buddy a bite of taco and enjoys a moment of peace.

I launch up onto the black walnut table suddenly appearing before the monkeys.

-Oh, hey.

They both say in unison and offer me a bit of taco.

And there you have the difference between cute and gorgeous.

Cute works, but gorgeous is easy.

I sit at the far end of the table and listen.

Clean.

They talk about family, friends, music, the weekend…

Sleep.

5

A pungent odor awakes me. I know that smell.

Sid has dried flower buds that reek like a skunk and he's cracked the mason-jar lid.

I charge off and get a good, long sniff up close.

The bouquet dances through my nostrils.

As much as I like the earthy smell of the buds; I despise the unmistakable burning odor. It's amazing how a little fire can transform something.

Sid passes the thin white cigarette to Victoria.

She releases a satisfied plume of smoke. It hypnotizes.

The movement, seduction, I charge only to stop short. It disappears and changes and…it's gone.

Victoria and Sid speak softly.

They inhale. They exhale deeply. They relax.

It's a toss-up- Continue gazing at the ever changing blue clouds

Or

Head upstairs to fresh air.

The room loses its appeal. I bolt.

I hear them laugh as I launch the staircase. They find the strangest things humorous. Isn't it obvious?

It stinks in here and I won't tolerate it.

Buddy sits between them on the couch. This is his favorite time.

He snuggles so close he actually sinks beneath them a bit. He pushes closer, rests his head on the brown leather couch, and exhales as if he has spent the day toiling away breaking boulders and is now finally able to rest his weary head.

I sit at the top of the steps.

Clean.

I hear cereal falling into a glass bowl. I am in the kitchen before the milk is poured. Buddy and I enjoy a crunchy bit each.

The smoke and smell have faded from the living room.

Victoria and Sid gorge themselves on cereal, but not the sugary unhealthy kind.

I settle on the couch just above Sid's head. Buddy's in his lap. Victoria's sitting with her legs resting on Sid's that are stretched out on the coffee table. An old movie from the 1950s is on- the one with the sad guy in the red jacket with the cigarette.

He's melodramatic but in the best way, so cool.

We fall asleep.

When I awake, it's time.

I leave my family snoring and splayed on the couch.

I slink to the kitchen and proceed down the familiar worn-rug steps.

A new hunt begins.

6

It's the weekend so the monkeys sleep later, talk over coffee, watch some television, and clean the entire house.

I jockey from room to room. I despise the vacuum and battle the broom.

All of the windows are open and I sniff, my eyes closed, nose in the air.

This is a rare and favorite time; the doors wide open.

I get an hour gazing through the full-length, glass door, plotting an escape.

Buddy trots around sniffing grass, oblivious to the sky and open space. He walks the backyard perimeter, lifts his leg a few times and settles in the sun, a long yawn then sleep.

I stare envious.

How could they trust this senseless mongrel outside and not I?

He doesn't even know how to exercise his freedom.

Buddy starts to sniff excitedly and then proceeds to roll in bird shit.

I've had enough; I saunter upstairs.

Fresh air?

I sprint to the attic. The windows are wide open and no screen!

Sid's wiry frame squirms out of the window and onto the roof; he's yelling something down to Victoria. A green garden hose appears.

He sprays the gutters.

The spray's mist carries earthy smells, signs of life-creepy, crawly, gutter life.

I'm on the roof. I'm looking at Sid's back. He's cursing. He has tattoos and freckles.

He rarely curses so I know he's angry. His neck is red.

He turns clutching his pale wrist. His sandal slips, the hose slides off the shingles, and he catches himself on his knees. He curses, crawls inside the window and stomps away.

He doesn't see me.

-Goddamn hornet!

The sink runs, steps up the stairs, question.

-Ouch!

Says Victoria when she enters the bathroom.

-Yep, hurts. Look how red and bumpy and white in the middle. Weird.

-Gross. You got the stinger?

- Yeah, sucker came outta nowhere. Didn't see a hive but I wouldn't be surprised.   Sucks.

-Go put some ice on it and sit down. You want somethin' ?

-Nah.

Steps downstairs.

Victoria enters the bedroom and closes the screens.

I'm on the roof.

I'm alone on the roof!

I crawl back to the white stucco and set myself in the corner next to the gutter.

I sit, stare, sniff, and blink.

I'm on the second floor. The breeze moves through my slender body. Late afternoon, and I watch the birds. This is my dream, my nature.

The darker it gets the more I awaken, my vision filed to a predator's point.

Everything slows down. The birds move by, I see every wing's thrust and flutter. Slowmotion.

I gaze at the pretty plumes, the golden browns, blues, and reds.

Blood red.

My lower lip trembles.

I smell Sid is at the grill. My mouth salivates.

The charcoal's cinders are slowly fading. I debate jumping down and coaxing a meal. It's tempting, but I relish my time outside. I've never been outside!

I continue taking it in, sensing the cadence, the primary quarry and more importantly fellow predators.

You'd think they'd miss me?

I'll get lost hunting in the basement for two days and they never see me.

I'm seen when I want to be.

Besides, the reaction of beaming joy I get from the monkeys when I suddenly appear is worth it.

I'm guaranteed bacon and a good scratch.

I usually carry a dead mouse, moth, or spider.

Victoria brushes off my flat snout, whiskers, and eyes.

-Gross. Kitten where have you been?

-She got another mouse; it's by the back door.

Yells Sid proudly. He appreciates my night's work.

He places the small, smooth gray mouse in a zip lock plastic bag and drops it in the garbage can outside.

The shingles cool.

The sun is down but the soft orange glow persists.

In the shadowy blue sky, black sporadic movements demand my attention.

Left, right, left right.

Like birds but move like butterflies. No feathers. The flapping never stops.

Skin.

I'm hypnotized.

Flying rodents!

They resemble torn pieces of black construction paper falling haphazardly from the sky.

I'm at the edge of the gutter. I stare, chatter, crouch, crouch, crouch, leap!

I catch one in my front paws as I fully extend my body reaching the apex of the hasty swan dive.

I pull the flying mouse in. All four paws squeeze the cupped creature as I begin to descend. The claws puncture, squeeze. I crush the hot throat. The animal goes limp. I release my prey, extend my legs like a skydiver, and prepare for impact. The second my paws feel the ground I transfer my weight, slide to the left, roll and pop up looking for my kill.

I hear squeaks and rustling.

Silence.

The rodent is dead.

As I make my way to the tiny corpse, I hear a gruff, growling, growing.

I spin forgetting the kill. I focus on the demonic sound emanating from the next door neighbor's fence. I advance slowly, belly to the ground.

The boundary is constructed of two-foot wide, white wooden planks. Between each plank is a two-inch space.

I stop short. I see a yellow eye watching me. I freeze.

A large, black silhouette with bristly fur appears as if raised from the ground.

We stare at each other.

The low growl persists- a dangerous click in its throat.

The yellow eye surprises me. It's patient. Two stone hunters locked on each other.

The animal is different than Buddy. It thrives outdoors, smells of leaves, grass, and mud. It's a hundred pounds, maybe more.

I attempt to locate a point of attack, a method in which to assassinate, but the fence obscures my line of sight.

-There you are!

Says Sid being led by an excited Buddy attached to a black leash with tiny white skulls.

-Victoria!

He yells into the open living room window.

-I found Baby Blue!

Buddy drags Sid by the taught leash. He gives me the once over with his flat, wet snout. I jab with my paw several times in succession. He wants to play, but I'm trying to push him out of my view.

Buddy suddenly barks and goes rigid. Listens. His hair rises. The yellow eye responds with a deep, powerful bellow. Buddy responds by throwing his entire compact body into every bark. His front paws bounce.

It's a chirp and ridiculous compared to the dog next door.

The growl continues.

-What are ya barkin' at? There's nothing there, Bud.

Says Sid as he tugs Buddy down the driveway.

Victoria scoops me up from behind. My hunter instincts falter due to my new discovery next door, Odin, the fellow predator. Somehow he's told me his name.

Sid and Buddy fade into the muggy night. Victoria carries me inside scolding all the way.

I can't see it, but I know the yellow eye is still watching, unblinking.

7

I'm bored. The monkeys watch a movie and Buddy snores. I launch in front of the television and block their view.

-Com'om, Blue. Really? Now?

-It's your turn.

Sid opens a small drawer in the living room coffee table.

I jump down with a thump and creep down, to the floor readying myself.

He retrieves a two-inch long, silver metal tube, like a keychain. He pushes the button and the red light appears.

It slides across the floor taunting me, the elusive prey.

It dances circles and figure eights on the dark green rug.

It captures me.

Hypnotized. The long red comet trails across the floor before my eyes.

I crouch, study, steady. Crouch, study steady.

I pounce! I have it! It's gone. I have it. It's gone. I…had…it?

The hunt continues. The glowing dot creeps up walls, watches from the ceiling, and buzzes around right before my paws. I use all of my senses, but it makes no sound, has no scent, only blood red illumination. I pursue and finally collapse in exhaustion. I soon saunter away retiring to my perch, a five-foot furry tower next to the couch. Sleep.

I know the monkeys control the red dot, but I'm convinced I can beat it. Win it. Kill it. Someday I'll capture it, but meanwhile, I revel in the chase. I dream of being engulfed by the glowing orb- red shimmering around and through me. Lifting me, I sail in my red comet.

8

I've been able to get passed the attic door. The old, heavy doorknob fell out when Sid was stung by the hornet. He hasn't noticed yet.

I push the door aside with my slender body and head up the stairs. I settle on the window sill facing the neighbors. It's uncomfortable at first, but I want to see Odin and his yellow eye. I settle on the splinter-lined sill. I gaze beyond the fence to the backyard. I spot a small vegetable garden, bird bath, and two wooden Adirondack lounge chairs.

As I lower my gaze, I see the yellow orb looking directly into my amber eyes.

I can't believe the size and shape of the dog, it's more a wolf. He's shiny, I could mistake him for a black bear, but the lonely yellow eye and pointy snout tell me otherwise.

He's sitting; mouth slightly open, sharp pointy teeth catch the sunlight.

His dangling, dark tongue gives the impression of a grin.

Is he smiling at me?

He rises to his great paws, stretches, shakes, and slowly walks around the yard.

I've never seen a beautiful dog before.

Sleep.

When I awake in the window, it's dusk and there is a headless groundhog in the middle of the yard. Odin is sleeping; his bristly fur pokes out from the white fence.

I'm in awe. I wish I witnessed the carnage; how didn't it wake me? A silent killer leaves a gift.

A gift for me?

9

Awful.

My monkeys are having a party and apparently it includes the guests' dogs.

2 hyper Italian Greyhounds, Dante and Leonardo motor up and down the yard yipping and yapping.

1 old German Shepard named Baron who's content laying in the shade with an occasional woof, stretch, yawn, and sleep.

1 Chinese crested who has a bit of reddish-brown hair sticking up haphazardly from his head, other than that he is completely hairless. He resembles an old man with sunspots and skinny stooped frame. His name is Freddy and he is the only other dog I can tolerate. Everyone loves Freddy. He is gentle and sincere like a sage or monk; his eyes shine. He also gets a great tan in the summer which is currently beginning to fade and peal.

Buddy introduces himself to each guest as they arrive.

He's a good host. Everyone laughs at the site of him. Children hug him and he'll gently sniff a newborn's head without waking it. I don't understand why or how he does it.

I hide upstairs on the monkey's bed. My attempt at slumber is constantly interrupted- barks, odors, and general white noise pull me awake.

Sid mans the grill and the music, constantly weaving inside and outside of the house.

Victoria welcomes, socializes, and accepts food and wine. She has many family members unlike Sid. Her family is constantly yelling, laughing, eating, and arguing. They all show up with food; there's always too much, so Victoria doesn't let anyone leave empty handed.

Buddy revels in the excitement, his senses on overload. He bounds around after each dog throwing his little barrel body. I watch him send the greyhounds flying like bowling pins.

I change location to the attic. I search for Odin. I know he's there, but I can't spot him, not even the yellow eye. I feel his presence. I need to find escape from the house again and when I do; I'm scaling the fence and meeting the beast face to face.

The day darkens, people leave; people arrive. I make a dash for the litter box. The monkeys' friends point in astonishment as the "blue blur" flies past them. Some attempt to grab, others marvel at me.

-Oh my God! The face.

-Beautiful.

-So fast.

- Where did she come from?

-You guys have a cat?

They're slow, clumsy monkeys so I bob, weave, and sprint my way past them with ease.

I visit the litter box.

Clean.

I prepare for the obstacle course back up to the attic, but

the small basement window grabs my attention. Two new dogs walk by.

They remind me of Buddy; the same flat mug and stocky build.

2 French bulldogs. The first named Andy is beautiful. He is snow white with glimpses of clean pink skin that he never lost from his puppy days.

Buddy lunges into the picture; his head low to the ground. Andy assumes the same posture. They take short hops back and forth until Andy breaks into a sprint for the backyard. Buddy follows Andy everywhere for the rest of the day. Sid jokes that Buddy wants to be Andy. He urinates and dumps in the same spots and he'll also sit and lick Andy's ears clean while he lounges in the sun. What Andy does, Buddy is sure to follow.

The other dog is solid black. He never barks and stays to himself.

He watches, listens, sniffs the air, but stays calm and focused.

He's not aggressive but pensive.

He allows monkeys to pet him; mongrels to sniff him, but he seems distracted, like he's concentrating on something else. He tolerates the interruptions without a lick or sniff.

His head is a bit too large for his stocky frame.

He's comprised of rippling muscles that flex with each step.

He lacks the cute, smooth, pink gut that Andy enjoys having rubbed.

I'm impressed with the dog.

His name is Ares.

I'm blindsided by two fat, pale hands!

A large, intoxicated brute picks me up.

He reeks of stale beer and cigarettes.

Instead of fleeing, I wrap my legs around his forearm and dig in my claws.

He runs upstairs shaking his limb as if it were on fire.

We enter the kitchen and everyone steps aside to gawk at the spectacle.

He doesn't realize that I can hang-on for as long as I choose. He swings his arm in a circle, but I balance with ease.

The partygoers double over with laughter.

-Ha! Look at Owen!

-Cat's a killer.

-I think he's starting to cry!

I release, catch flight, land on the hardwood floor, and prance off satisfied with my lesson. The room erupts with laughter, but I'm already on the master bed licking my paws clean.

Sleep.

10

I'm worried about my monkeys. They're always stressed about finances. I sense when the storm is building to an argument. The voices change cadence and pitch. Long before the actual yelling begins, I'm under the monkeys' bed avoiding the battle.

The hollering sounds like shrieks to my ears. There is no physical altercation, but I wonder if that would finally settle disputes like it does for me. If I'm confronted, I simply snap the neck of my opponent and go to sleep satisfied. Today the argument lasts many minutes. Buddy cowers on the couch watching, waiting, wining.

Sid storms out followed by Victoria. They part ways for the morning commute without a kiss or goodbye.

They leave the television on for Buddy all day, but he sleeps while I pay attention even when I'm in slumber. I can't help it; my ears gather the sounds that surround me in case of attack.

Monkeys make no sense.

Heads on the screen speak but say nothing.

Monkeys act but nothing gets accomplished; they're so slow. The television blares away. I drift off.

I know when people are lying.

The television is a liar.

When I was on the roof the other day, I took the time to survey the neighborhood.

In every house- a constant blue, blinking, ever-changing light.

They fall asleep listening and watching; their eyes closed.

How do they rest? What do they experience behind their eyelids?

The monkeys worship liars. For some reason they're popular.

I leave the living room and head down to the basement. I don't know why the monkeys are stressed; their lives never appear to be in danger. Their worries never happen. They're in constant but different states of fear. Instead of simply conquering or killing whatever this fear is, they ignore it.

Monkeys fill themselves with something else to take up the time. Anything but actually facing whatever scares them. They don't realize how much harder they make it by lying to themselves or ignoring that pesky problem.

When the darkness comes and the demons come out, they are victims of themselves.

They're in denial.

I'm not.

I decide life and death.

I walk a warrior's path.

I live to die.

I don't hesitate, complain, lie, or worry.

I hunt and kill, efficiently, cleanly.

It's what I am, so it will be done well.

I'm pure.

I don't think monkeys know who they are or what they're doing. They go out of their way to avoid being alone.

They expend all of their energy accomplishing nothing, and when it comes time to sleep; they can't

How do they dream?

Sleep.

11

Buddy and I got into one serious altercation the first year I moved in.

Sid and Victoria take turns feeding us.

Sid is in a hurry, careless, and sloppy.

Victoria is meticulous and neat.

Therefore feeding times were confusing until Buddy and I accepted the monkey's methods and personalities.

This particular day Victoria fed us.

Sid awoke late for work.

He stumbled through his morning routine blurry eyed and

Zombie-like. He brewed strong black coffee and departed wrinkled; cowlicks rhythmically bobbing in his wake.

He neglected to close the door; fired the engine; popped the brake; cranked the gear; and accelerated fading gravel treads.

I was hungry.

Buddy's belly grumbled. His black nails clicked on the hardwood floor announcing impatience.

I sat on the counter, compact and diligent, watching Victoria scrub the kitchen trying to catch her eye while she hummed softly.

The television filled the background. Buddy added wining to his pitiful tapping.

Any longer and he'd start to pace and grumbling.

Finally, Victoria filled our bowls with food but somehow mixed them up. I realized this but Buddy didn't have a clue. He'd gladly eat any food where as my diet is of a much more delicate nature.

When we simultaneously approached the same bowl, our hair raised. A switch was thrown. We launched at each other. Victoria described it later to Sid.

-It was like, when the cartoons merge into a fight and there's stars and a dust cloud. It was just like that, so fast. Unbelievable.

Victoria threw herself between us. Buddy launched again to bite, but Victoria's arm was the unfortunate recipient- a few drops of blood and a nasty bruise.

Victoria drew her arm back and Buddy deflated. His ears and tail went down and he cowered to the floor. Big black pug eyes looked up from that flat face and you couldn't help but love him.

Victoria yelled and he shot out of the room.

I sat their panting through my mouth. Listening.
Calculating. I was still in the red.

-Hey kitten, *relax*.

I couldn't. I ran downstairs to hunt whatever I could
find.

One June bug and three spiders later, Victoria told me
to never attack Buddy. She brought him over. He was
in her lap. She raised his pitiful arms. Cat scratches
crisscrossed his little bulging chest. I drew close and
sniffed the newly cleansed wounds. It was good work.
Buddy's lucky I didn't gauge out one of his eyeballs
or bite off one of his silky smooth ears.

We've been housemates ever since, not exactly
friends.

I don't have friends.

12

Instinct gets me into trouble.

Sid gives me catnip. The fragrance calls and dances in my mind. My insides swell and ignite gushing warmth, like velvety blood.

I pounce on the dry green bud attempting to embrace, fuel, and live with the ecstasy forever. I roll engulfing my essence with the seductive smell attempting to fill every cell with the potent plant.

I'm lost.

I'm gone.

Normally, I'm calculated. But when the emerald herb is presented, I'm possessed. I do what I normally would not.

I lay on my back sliding my head to my tail back and forth, a brushing rhythm.

This would normally be humiliating. It's childish and risky. But I don't care. I don't think.

I feel.

I stare at the black blurring blades attached to the ceiling fan.

It expands, lowers just before my eyes.

Blades blowing before my dazzled amber orbs tell me a tale.

I plunge into the whirling cyclone and immerse myself in its story.

Meanwhile my body lays prone stone still on my back, while the true me is gone.

I'm the spirit floating through the ether. Soaring. Stalking.

I hunt stars in the sky. Obliterate planets. Eviscerate hawks and vultures.

I fly through the sun. I emerge from the great star blasting across the black abyss plunging into the ocean.

The deep dark, drink surges carrying me in its tide. Normally I despise water, but here I'm the master.

I expand- the great new predator, hunting specter. I stretch my claws surrounding it all, clutching the world. I send it blasting, breaking, beating through to the other side.

It's suddenly bright and quiet.

I awake on the warm wooden floor but don't move a muscle. I barley breathe.

It's dark outside. The small kitchen window light is the only beacon.

The catnip fever fantasy fades as I wake. Soon it will be lost.

I take a long drink and swat at Buddy's curly tale when he decides he needs a drink too.

The slight oppressive hangover sets in. I'm as lost as my wandering, wondering monkeys.

I'm depleted.

Sleep.

13

At first I smell mold and moth balls. Instinct has me sprinting from the kitchen to the dining room and finally underneath the brown leather living room couch.

I pull into a tight ball and sit still. I watch Sid's boat shoes stomping back and forth and up and down; all the while calling-

-"Blue?"

-Baby Blue, wanna treat?

-Little Blue, where are you?

I know better.

The moldy, mothball odor is the pink crate used to shuffle me to the veterinarian's.

It stinks and has only a cheap, old, terry cloth towel for comfort and some lame toy like a fuzzy mouse or rubber fish. It's stored in the attic and rarely used but I hate it all the same.

People talk about freedom on television. Sacrifice for freedom. Fight for freedom.

But I doubt any of them have been grabbed by the scruff of the neck and forced into a bubblegum colored cage. Then again they never know what true freedom is anyway.

It's futile.

Sid catches up with me and stuffs me into the tiny pink jail. I don't make it easy for him. I silently bite and scratch, while keeping my limbs outstretched delaying the unavoidable defeat.

I attempt to sleep on the car ride, but the ever changing outside puts me on alert. I can't relax.

Sid parallel parks and picks up the crate on the passenger seat. I turn my back to him. He opens the car door and I'm hit with fresh air and cacophony. I peak through the holes on the back of the cage and access the environment to no avail.

The vet is a large man with a pointy chin. He's gentle and nice; I hear his deep voice, but I'm still in the crate. He unlatches the top and lifts the lid.

The room is bright and a blend of odors. I try to pinpoint the dominant scent which is a dog's, but the nurse wipes the stainless steel table with rubbing alcohol.

The odor bites, burns and obliterates any living smells. He scoops me up and cradles me like a child. He's learned from my sharp claws that this is the way I prefer to be held.

He takes my temperature, weight, and vitals. It was just a check-up but I'm glad to be leaving. The vet always trims my claws and the extra fur that catches gunk around my large amber eyes. I'll soon be comfortable in the old house.

Sid pays and carries me out. He places me on the passenger seat. He lashes his belt and we're off. He doesn't turn on the radio and I appreciate that. I enjoy the dominant, single thrumming of the car's engine. It's one of those little hatchbacks- a 5-speed. Sid shifts gears to the rise and rhythm of the transmission. We settle in 5th on the highway and cruise in the left lane.

I doze off.

A blaring horn shakes my body. My heart is pounding. Sid is silent. The blast continues to ring through the vehicle. I hear the tires screech above the general noise; then a hissing sound as the car begins to slide sideways on the grassy median. The burnt rubber smell hits me just as the pink prison is launched into the windshield cracking it. It finally bounces, and settles underneath the front passenger seat. I'm upside down and perfectly still. I fear if I make a move I'll cause more destruction.

Silence.

The door opens and the beeping signal begins indicating the door is ajar.

I hear footsteps running. I smell burning from the locked tires and the 40 yard slide between the highways.

Three long screams rip through the air above the beeping door signal.

Sid's primal scream.

I hear horns blare and somebody yelling and another laughing as they pass by. It all sounds muffled and blurry, coming and going.

Running footsteps approach the car. Sid jumps into the car and my prison is lifted from under the passenger seat.

He smells of vomit and is ashen. His hands shake as he pulls me out of the cracked plastic crate. He pulls me into his chest and hugs me tightly. Some of the sick is on his gray zip-up hoody.

I'm already calm and settled. I've surveyed and accepted the situation. I'm fine but monkeys are dumb and clumsy. He's in a panic and holds me to his chest. The car is about one yard away from the beginning of a concrete guard rail.

He calms. I push my paws to get some breathing room.

He's different, tense. He smells of sour sweat. His heart is pounding; hands shaking; and he's standing their holding me like a baby.

We're between two roaring highways with vehicles moving faster than I ever thought possible. Sid walks a few steps beyond the car, stops, faces the setting sun and begins to laugh and cry.

I smell soap, a clean spicy fresh sent. It wafts over Sid's shoulder from the artificial wind created by the constant hissing of the traffic.

-Ya'll alright?

A smooth southern voice emerges like a song.

Sid spins around to face a large black man in a baseball cap and expensive gold glasses. He has a toothpick in the corner of his mouth. He wears a light tan suit with no tie. It bellows in the wind and he slowly surveys the car, taking out the toothpick as he begins to speak.

-Don't seem to be any damage. Paints gonna need work though.

He says motioning with the tooth pick than placing it back into his mouth.

He finally looks to us. Sid doesn't move or say a word. He stares with a few tears still left on his cheeks.

-Ya'lls lucky. You show you okay?

He says as he takes the toothpick back out of his mouth.

He approaches Sid, but his sunglasses are focused on me. He tips the sunglasses to the tip of his nose revealing clear black eyes. He's a handshake's distance from us.

-What inna worls zat?

He says looking right at me as Sid cradles me.

-Oh yeah. Hey, um thanks for stopping. Shit man, I thought she died.

He says lifting me a bit. Then looking down and shaking his head.

-Thought I died too.

He adds as an afterthought.

He surveys the car but really he's just staring off still lost.

The man advances. He sticks out his large fist for me to smell as an introduction. I appreciate that. I smell cologne and skin cream like pine and winter. We push into each other and he begins scratching behind my ears and the side of my flat face. I jump into his arms.

-Wo. She likes you, man. And she doesn't like anyone, not even me.

Says Sid arms still open.

The large bear of a man lets out a laugh so high, it sounds like a little girl.

-Look at *you* lil' lady. Calm and cool as can be.

He continues to rub my ears and belly. His huge right hand rubs my entire undercarriage as he holds my entirety in his left palm.

-Hey, thanks for stoppin'.

-Not a problem, jus glad you okay. You know what's coo though, dis kitten. She one coo-kee-cat.

He says shaking his head and smiling.

-Man. Look at dat face. Never seen nothin' like it.

Sid looks at me in the giant man's arms as if he never saw me before. He shakes his head and smiles. The sweet smelling man gently hands me back to Sid.

-See ya'll later.

He said giving one last tug on my ear.

-Yeah. Thanks again.

We watch the large man get into his shiny SUV and accelerate away.

-Let's go home Coo-kee-cat.

14

I really should have seen in it coming. It's laughable really.

I reminisce and smile. I know you'll find that strange.

I lost. And that's okay, just fine. It was a glorious end.

An epic battle that's now ended and I'm dead.

I'm the same "energy". I feel mostly the same, but I can move faster. I think of a place and I'm suddenly there.

I'm hovering above the broken husk that used to be me.

I really do look blue.

It's shocking how different I look.

I felt like a tiger.

But this poor crumpled creature before me is not what I imagined. It's not a tiger.

It's tiny and sad.

I see Sid and Victoria embraced. They squeeze like white knuckles.

Both breathe with sobs.

Sid glances at the dead cat on the silver tray; looks to the floor; doubles the hug and draws Victoria even closer.

Victoria never shows her face and that's fine.

She doesn't want to remember me as a two year old cat with a broken neck.

I understand that they're sad, but I'm not.

I had crept over to visit Odin. Upon entering the gated yard, I scanned for the hellhound. For such a large dog, he had an amazing ability to disappear and blend in with the background. Even with my keen night vision, it would take me several minutes to pinpoint the exact location of the floating yellow eye.

The large, looming, bristly, black form took shape. His massive head was on the soft dark grass. I crawled on my belly until we were nose to nose.

Silence.

The yellow eye hovered before me.

The same wolf smile.

The same earthy smell.

I'd never been this close to him before. I assumed he would radiate heat like a big, black oven, but the air was thin and cold. Two jets of mist shot out of his huge frosty snout. The smile showed teeth. Rows upon rows of tiny white triangles created to tear. Black and pink gums raised and lowered revealing molars created to crush.

This was not a dog of our century. It's one of the wild dogs the Greeks feared so much. Like the black, bitches chasing sinners through the dark wood breaking thorny branches. Dismembering. Walking away triumphantly with a limb held high in the air. That's the type of dog Odin was.

I waited for my instinct to take over, but the switch was absent. I felt great. I felt light and full. I tingled and smiled. I grinned until it hurt, nose to nose with the hellhound.

I sat and stared as the ice-box mouth began to slowly open.

White, sharp teeth. Black and pink gums.

I should have lashed out and destroyed this, but it felt too good.

I was drawn in. I stepped onto the beast's wide-open gaping mouth. It was cool and still like a marble sculpture. It smelt of cold snowy weather. My nostrils burned as I drew in the comforting clean smell. It was so distinct and rare.

I lay on the purple tongue with my paws tucked under me.

The mouth snapped shut.

Sleep.

15

I awoke on the hardwood living room floor in the sun.
The warm rays felt good. I got up to stretch, but there
was nothing to stretch. I existed but it was energy. I
hovered about the house with ease.

I could imagine being on the roof and then I was on
the roof.

I was at my full potential.

It was thrilling.

I shot into Sid and Victoria's bedroom and lay
between them.

-Hey!

-Com'on Buddy!

The dog charged out from under the light-blue down
comforter.

He huffed, snorted and barked.

Victoria got up to pee. I plopped down onto the white
and black tile. She sat with her face in her hands, eyes
puffy and bloodshot.

She had no idea I was there. Buddy burst open the
door and sprang right at me. I hovered to the ceiling
and zoomed around the tiles.

-Dog's gone crazy.

Called Victoria to a sleeping Sid, while getting up and flushing.

Buddy stared at the ceiling.

I've found that I can travel anywhere I imagine.

I've been exploring for what I think is days, but it could be months or years.

I'm on a different plane, a different dimension. Animals can see me, especially dogs and birds. At first they are disturbed, but once they catch my cold snowstorm scent, they relax and forget I'm there.

Oh, I forgot!

You probably want the specifics on my death.

Humans are scared of death. They ignore it with denial and illusion. They fill the cold lonely place that reminds them late at night that no matter what they do, each living being is ultimately alone.

It's a sobering darkness that screams only once in a while, but it's deafening, and it brings tears and clenched clothing from hugs that can't be too tight, words that can't be too comforting. Soon it calms to a murmur, then a whisper, and then an unpleasant distant dream. And then it's gone.

That's how they keep on going.

I was killed.

The monkeys had another party and several of the guests spent the night. As a result, the festivities wore on into the early dark morning. The remaining stumbled around looking for a comfortable place to sleep. Most of the beds and couches were taken with snoring slumber.

The French bulldogs were spending the night because Owen got too drunk to drive. Penny, his girlfriend, was home sick with food poisoning, which turned out to be morning sickness for her undetected pregnancy. Andy and Ares were in the basement with the door closed. They had plenty of room, nothing was breakable, and it was better than risking a mess in a bedroom.

Soon the house was quiet. Everyone was asleep except me. This was my prime hunting time. I crept down from the safe haven of the attic.

I was hungry.

I padded down the steps in the dark house and had a long drink.

I cleaned and stared at the basement door. Something was behind it.

Whatever it was, it was unwanted in my house. My predator's urge tightened my body into a coil. I smelt a dog and he smelled me. He gently scratched the door and snuffed loudly. I sat and waited.

Owen got up to urinate. His eyes were puffy slits in the early morning light.

He entered the kitchen, but turned left instead of right and almost stepped on me. He mistakenly opened the cellar door expecting the bathroom. A black shadow burst through the opening as Owen turned the knob and pulled.

I was already in the air claws out. We crashed together- black and blue.

Owen tripped down the basement steps spraining his ankle.

Andy was confused and barking up the steps, but didn't know where to go.

God, he was stronger and much faster than I expected. We both lunged for the throat. Our mussels met teeth to teeth causing a white flash before my eyes. I think Owen was screaming but my bloodlust had me rapt.

Ares bit my neck and held tight shaking me like a ragdoll. I brought all four paws up

to his chest and face slicing and gauging. I felt no pain. My body's smart and knows how to protect me from agony. We growled and doubled our efforts. I was able to free my neck as he opened his mouth to get a better grip. I bit into his throat and wrapped my claws around his large black head.

I don't recall the rest. I awoke on the kitchen counter. Sunlight was coming through the window. I smelt blood and urine. I heard sobs.

-I found her! She's okay!

Hollered Sid to the search party.

He gently lifted and cradled me. I couldn't feel anything.

Victoria sprinted into the kitchen. She went to hold me, but drew back in fear. I looked a mess and smelt vile. My neck was broken and I knew I was dead but I couldn't leave Victoria yet. I held on and she wept. I wanted to move on to the next stage but we needed to say goodbye. I could hear the calling but ignored it for now. It was the next way and natural but Victoria's shock and sadness held me in my broken body.

I opened my eyes and saw a black dog with a head too large for his body. He was bleeding on the kitchen floor. Owen was kneeling down holding a kitchen towel to his mussel. I glanced at my sticky front paws and saw it in all of its glory- Ares's bloody eyeball. I smiled. He may have killed me, but I left my mark.

He'll never forget.

He'd have his left eye socket sewn shut at the vet while I got X-rays. He would go on and live, while I prepared for my next life.

Sleep.

16

My next memory is going over to Odin and climbing into his nebulous mouth. All that time I thought we would battle and it turns out he was my guide to the next world.

My body was eventually cremated.

When I entered that chilly mouth I was at peace.

I learned humans can't see me.

When I awoke, I was no longer in the clean cool winter mouth. I was in Victoria's dream. We were walking toward each other on curly white fog.

She stopped short and gasped.

She didn't move a muscle.

She didn't breathe.

She was worried I would disappear.

I leapt an enormous distance and landed softly in her arms. She beamed bringing our faces together. She cradled me like a baby.

-Ah, my beautiful Blue. My coo-kee-cat.

She exhaled relieved and satisfied.

We were warm.

We were breathing in unison.

We stayed like that for a long time.

When she awoke, I was gone.

She was a little bit lighter, a little less sad.

I hope she knows I'm safe and waiting. I visit her dreams whenever I can.

Occasionally, I'll hop into Sid's dreams too. We don't hug or touch. I bop by in the background. It always brings a smile to his face. Sometimes he gives me the thumbs up. Other times a peace sign. I hope he knows I'm waiting for him too.

17

I still hunt. Actually, I'm stalking my prey right now. I've been watching him the past few days through his bedroom window. He's seen me from his bed gazing out the window never knowing if I'm a reality or not.

He's standing at the window looking into my amber eyes. I enter the room and rub up on his legs. He's confused but feels incredible. Anything would feel better than the cancer eating away at his lungs and bones.

But he's not a prisoner of that broken-down shell anymore. He's moved onto the next stage and starting to realize it. Sometimes it takes a little while to convince the souls to follow. He finally scoops me up and I transport us outside to the road by the river. He's astonished and laughing.

We shine.

-I guess I'm following' you lil' lady.

He says with a delighted chuckle.

My instinct is sharp but guided differently.

I stalk people who are on their deathbed. They receive comfort from their pain when they observe me through a window or in a dream. When the time is right, I spring on them and become their guide.

The Egyptians knew this. They revered cats.

The Anglo-Saxons and Celts knew it was ravens- one on each of Odin's shoulders and the morrigon.

The Greeks and Romans knew it too, but got it a bit confused hence Cerberus and the dreaded hellhounds.

The more noise the world creates, the further the monkeys get away from the earth's energy and instinct. It's the phenomenon some monkeys call God.

But we don't have the capability to even begin to comprehend something so massive.

It can only be experienced.

It doesn't matter where, the river's always there.

I lead them to the same place. I'm not the only one with this duty.

Dogs and ravens take part in the salvation hunt.

The dogs lead those who die during the day.

The ravens lead anyone who has passed on outside.

The cats lead those who expire at night.

I don't make sense of it. It is my instinct so I know it's correct. I walk down the road with the man. We listen to the river. He soon learns to his amusement that he can hover and zoom around faster than he's ever traveled. He dips and dives glowing like a star.

He continues following, always behind me. The world looks the same except a bit brighter and clearer. Everything is crisp. There is no confusion or noise. This is the time of rest and rejuvenation.

We come to a hill. We ascend with anticipation. As we reach the peak, we can see only darkness. This is my favorite part.

As we take the last step, we look down on a million fireflies.

There's a glorious sound.

Like a crackling fire.

Like wind through the trees.

Like the crashing ocean.

Like the clip-clop of horse's hooves.

Like the rushing river.

Like a song bird's tune.

Like the rain.

Like sleep.

I smile.

Souls from every living thing zip around embracing.

Celebrating. Dancing. Tails wag. Cats leap. Birds soar. Angels sing.

This continues for a minute or a year. Who can be sure and who really cares?

Time has no business here.

Eventually we settle our rhythms and vibrations; they pulse in unison. We gaze at the purple mountains in the distance. A fissure of silver light highlights the jagged line.

The sky dims dark blue to black.

In an instant, the sky is full of more stars than we can fathom.

We gaze in silent awe.

The stars descend.

Closer, larger, brighter.

They merge and fuse into one massive starlight.

We plunge into a new life as the stars rain down joining us all together.

It's beautiful and perfect.

Sleep.

When I awake, I'm before my prey and the glorious cycle begins anew.

I wish I could tell Victoria and Sid not to worry. I wish I could tell them things still go on.

They got a new kitten. It's a puffy white Persian with big blue eyes. It's hardly a hunter. She's more of a lounger, created to look beautiful. Her purrs are songs. She chases the red light but gives up too soon. She is stroked by the lucky few.

She's soft and warm, just what they need.

She gets annoyed by the ever present, always demanding Buddy, but tolerates him too.

Sometimes I shoot through like a blue comet, an azure phantom and give her a thrill.

But she is no coo-kee-cat.

Sometimes they talk about me laughing. They say I was like James Dean- I had to die young, "the immortal cool" as Sid puts it.

Sometimes Sid wishes he drew me more.

Sometimes Victoria secs me, but blinks and I'm gone.

Sometimes they forget me altogether. That's good. That's surviving. That's instinct.

Besides, we all meet again in the end.

Made in the USA
Lexington, KY
25 January 2012